Dracula
and
Frankenstein
Are Friends

by Katherine Tegen

illustrated by Doug Cushman

Dracula

Frankenstein

HarperCollinsPublishers

Dracula and Frankenstein Are Friends
Text copyright © 2003 by Katherine Brown Tegen
Illustrations copyright © 2003 by Doug Cushman
Manufactured in China. All rights reserved.
www.harperchildrens.com

Library of Congress Cataloging-in-Publication Data
Tegen, Katherine Brown.
  Dracula and Frankenstein are friends / by Katherine Brown Tegen ;
illustrated by Doug Cushman.—1st ed.
    p. cm.
  Summary: Dracula and Frankenstein are friends until they both decide to
have a Halloween party.
  ISBN 0-06-000115-1 — ISBN 0-06-000116-X (lib. bdg.)
  [1. Friendship—Fiction. 2. Monsters—Fiction. 3. Halloween—Fiction.
4. Parties—Fiction.] I. Cushman, Doug, ill. II. Title.
PZ7.T22964 Dr 2003   2002014461
[E]—dc21   CIP
                                                            AC

Typography by Matt Adamec
1 2 3 4 5 6 7 8 9 10
❖
First Edition

To my own little monsters—
Tyler and Charlotte

—K.B.T.

For Jeffy and Pepo

—D.C.

Dracula and Frankenstein are friends. They live in two side-by-side houses, in a town where all of the houses are spooky.

This is Dracula's house.

He likes to keep the rooms dark during the day.

Bats are his buddies. He sleeps in a coffin, of course.

This is Frankenstein's house.
Up in the attic, Frankenstein's electrical
conductor captures lightning every time it storms.
Frankenstein's favorite room is the laboratory,
where he performs scientific experiments. His
assistant helps him, most of the time.

Dracula has lived for a long, long time in his house.
He gets bored easily. He'll often say to Frankenstein,
"Variety is the spice of life." And then he and Frankenstein
will mess around with some other monster toys.

Some days Dracula shares his other favorite mottoes: "All work and no play makes Dracula a dull boy" and "Nice guys finish last." Then, watch out!

Frankenstein admires Dracula for his tricky ways and clever ideas. Once in a while, he has a good idea himself, but he's a shy kind of guy. He might not share it.

The Creepy Café is their favorite hangout for lunch.
Dracula and Frankenstein were both having tuna fish on rye
when Frankenstein said, "I might have a party this Halloween."

"Great idea!" said Dracula. "What's the theme?
What about entertainment? Music? Decorations?"

"Well, I was thinking of just a regular Halloween party," said Frankenstein. "You know, bobbing for apples, jack-o'-lanterns, candy, costumes."

Dracula closed his eyes. "Oh, yes, that could be good, that could be good. . . ." Dracula opened one eye. "I might have a party myself," he said.

Frankenstein was silent.

"I'd been thinking about having one, actually," said Dracula. "And most of our friends are different anyway."

"NOT!" said Frankenstein.

"Oh, well, be that way," said Dracula, and glided out of the café.

Frankenstein went home and made invitations. He
put them in his mailbox.

Dracula went home and made invitations, too.
Then he saw Frankenstein's invitations in
Frankenstein's mailbox.

Somehow, Dracula's invitations appeared in Dracula's
mailbox, and Frankenstein's disappeared.

A week later, it was Halloween.

Frankenstein carved dozens of pumpkins with funny
faces. He filled a big caldron with water and apples, and he
made prizes for the best costumes.

He sat down to wait for his monster friends.

The theme of Dracula's party was Rock Through
the Ages: Dress Up as Your Favorite Dead Person.
He had hired the hottest ghoul band.

Dracula planned to perform his own stand-up comedy act during a musical break.

The table was full of tasty snacks like eye-of-newt cupcakes and bat-wing pizza. The punch bowl was filled with fizzy red punch.

An hour later, the band was banging. The guests were
grooving. They were dressed as Julius Caesar, Abraham
Lincoln, Beethoven, Marie Antoinette, and Elvis Presley.
     The party was popping when Dracula happened to peer
through the window.

Frankenstein's house flickered with the light from the
jack-o'-lanterns. Frankenstein was still sitting in the living room.
"Ah, well, that's the way the cookie crumbles," mumbled
Dracula to himself.
He was dancing the funky chicken with Marie Antoinette,
but he kept looking out the window. The party had lost its fizz.

"Hmmm. I suppose charity begins at home," said Dracula.

"Cut!" he shouted into the mike.

"Now, everyone, the best is yet to be. Follow me."

The band packed up, and everyone tiptoed out the back door.
Dracula led the way.

The party was popping again when Frankenstein slapped
Dracula on the back and said, "Great party, huh?"
"But, of course," said Dracula. . . .

"What are friends for?"